THE TIME DETECTIVES

THE CURSE OF
CASTLE
CRANSTON

ALEX WOOLF

FICTION
EXPRESS

What do other readers think?

Here are some comments left on the Fiction Express blog about this book:

"I really enjoyed your Cranston Castle book. I am looking forward to your next books."
James, Norwich

"Could you write a second book to Castle Cranston? It was so good and I was gutted the book ended."
Ethan, Ludlow

"It really got me hooked. The plot was brilliant. Thanks for writing such a good ending."
Millie, North Walsham

"I loved your Curse of Castle Cranston *book as I found it terribly exciting."*
JT, Derbyshire

"The Curse of Castle Cranston *is a good book. It is very adventurous and I like that sort of idea."*
Gabriella, London

Contents

Cast of Main Characters

Here is a list of the main characters that appear in this book:

Joe and Maya, Time-travelling detectives

Lord Robert Mackenzie, Earl of Cranston

Sir William Mackenzie, son and heir to the Earl

Lady Ada Hamilton, widowed sister of Lord Robert

Sir James Hamilton, her son

Sir Archibald, Steward to Lord Robert

The Constable

Joanna, Lady-in-Waiting to Lady Hamilton

Lord Ewan, Earl of Athelbane, Lord Robert's mortal enemy

Father Dalliel, the castle Chaplain

The Tramp

The castle Physician

To my father, who is as brave as any medieval knight

Chapter 1

The Curse

"What was that noise?" whispered Maya. Her cousin Joe glanced nervously behind him. "What noise?" he asked.

They were standing on a hilltop in the middle of the wild Scottish countryside amidst the ruins of a castle. Its craggy walls and turrets were so old and worn they almost seemed part of the hill.

"Perhaps it was an animal… Joe suggested, or the wind."

"No, it was a sort of muttering sound," said Maya, "like someone talking to themselves."

Joe shivered. He couldn't imagine what sort of person would hang around in this sinister pile of ancient stones and he didn't fancy sticking around to find out. They'd come to Scotland for a relaxing walking holiday. But he knew from experience that holidays with Maya were rarely uneventful. This evening, for example, she'd insisted they explore the ruin.

"Perhaps we should head back to the campsite," said Joe. "It's getting pretty dark."

Maya ignored him. She was in full explorer mode now, peering up at the crumbling, moss-covered walls and turrets and checking out hidden alcoves. They were in what Joe reckoned had once been the great hall. The roof was long gone, but he could see a hollow area that must have housed an enormous fireplace.

"I think the noise came from over here," said Maya, heading through an archway into a darker area beyond.

"Be careful!" hissed Joe, but again she ignored him. Taking a deep breath, he followed her.

They entered a small room with high walls. Grass and weeds grew thickly underfoot and thorny brambles scraped at their jeans. In the centre of the room a rectangular stone emerged from the dense carpet of vegetation. Maya peered at its flat surface. "There's something written here," she said.

Joe's curiosity was aroused. He joined her by the stone, tracing the carved letters with his fingertips. It was too dark to read them, so he took out his torch and shone it on the pale surface. The words were just about legible:

The bones of Lord Robert here recline
Last of the Mackenzie Line
The malediction thus foretold
On page of black and ink of gold
A chalice stolen from his hands
There came a blight upon his lands
With the coming of Lord Ewan
His castle fell to wrack and ruin

"What does it mean?" gasped Maya. "What's a malediction?"

"I think it's like a curse," said Joe. "This bloke, Lord Robert, was buried here – and it says a chalice was stolen from him…."

"Maybe that's what unleashed the curse," speculated Maya. "Or maybe–"

She was interrupted by a low growl, coming from the undergrowth behind them.

Joe was so shocked he dropped the torch. It fell with a clatter on the stone and went out, plunging them into near darkness.

"What was that?!" groaned Maya.

Joe was paralysed with fear, too scared to turn around and face whatever was there – which was like no animal he'd ever heard. Could it be Lord Mackenzie coming back to life and seeking revenge?

"Let's get out of here," he managed to croak, and they started to back very slowly towards the arched entrance. Before they'd gone two paces, the growl sounded again, only this time much louder and closer. Joe's blood froze. His hands were crushed into tight fists.

Then, to his amazement, Maya started to laugh.

"That sounded more like a snore to me," she said.

Now he thought about it, she was right.

They turned and trod warily through the grass in the direction the sound had come from. A figure was lying there, almost invisible in the shadows. As they approached, another howling snore echoed around the high walls.

The sleeper turned out to be a young man with a slim face and grey, stubbly cheeks. He was dressed in a tatty old suit and tie.

"It's just a tramp," sighed Joe.

Suddenly, the man's eyes flipped open – they were a startlingly pale blue. "Visitors?" he said. "Och, I was not expecting visitors at this hour. I expect you'll be wanting the tour?"

Joe was stunned. Even Maya was lost for words as they watched him get to his feet and dust himself down.

"Welcome to Castle Cranston," he said grandly, "ancestral home of the Mackenzie clan… until 1270, when the castle was destroyed and the family wiped out. Any questions so far? Good! In that case, if you'll follow me, we'll start with the Outer Court and the Barbican." He began heading out of the little chamber.

"Wait!" said Maya.

The man stopped.

"What do you mean the castle was destroyed and the family wiped out? What happened?" She indicated the rectangular stone. "It mentions here something about a malediction."

"Which we think means 'curse'," added Joe.

The man heaved a heavy sigh and turned to face them. "Aye, it means curse alright," he said. "The chalice belonged to this castle, you see. It was made of pure gold and dated back to the very earliest years of the Scottish Church. But there was a curse attached to it, written in gold ink on black parchment. The curse stated that if this chalice was ever removed from the chapel, the castle would fall. Well, the chalice *was* removed."

"When?" asked Maya.

"Well, lassie, legend has it the loss was discovered on the fifth of September in the year 1270… Now, I reckon somebody stole it!"

"Who?" asked Joe.

"No one will ever know," replied the man. "But one thing's for sure – its loss caused terror in the castle. Lord Robert Mackenzie, Fifth Earl of Cranston, was convinced he was cursed and that ruination would follow… and he was right. Within days, his son and heir, Sir William, was dead – poisoned, they say – and the castle was put under siege by the forces of the ruthless Lord Ewan, Earl of

Athelbane. Cranston surrendered after barely a fight. Athelbane razed the castle to the ground, killing all its inhabitants, and that was that for the Mackenzies of Cranston. They disappeared from history."

"Was the chalice ever found?" asked Maya.

The man shook his head. "It was never seen again. Exactly what happened to it remains a mystery."

"A mystery worth investigating," said Joe, exchanging a glance with Maya.

"Good luck to you, my wee friends," chuckled the man. "Historians have been searching for the Cranston Chalice for centuries. I'm not sure what a couple of bairns can do…."

"Let's just say our methods are a little different," said Maya mysteriously.

The tramp noticed Joe taking a smartphone out of his pocket, and smiled.

"I doubt you'll be getting any signal up here, laddie."

"Will you excuse us a moment," Joe said. "We'd like to start our investigations now, if that's okay."

"Be my guests," laughed the tramp, and he watched them head back into the great hall. "But don't be too long now. I'm a busy man."

What the tramp didn't realize was that Joe's smartphone did a lot more than make calls and search the Internet. It could also take Joe and Maya on journeys through time.

As soon as they were out of earshot, Joe said: "1270… we've never been that far back before."

"I know," said Maya, her eyes shining in the fading light. "But wouldn't it be exciting to solve the mystery of this age-old curse?"

Joe had to agree – after all, it combined his two favourite things, history and detective work. "Let's find a smaller room, though," he said. "Appearing in the great hall during a feast would not be the best start. This is the Middle Ages after all. They'll accuse us of being witches and burn us, or something."

He led her into a smaller room on the far side of the hall, then switched on the phone. The screen lit up:

Hello Joe Smallwood. Which time would you like to visit?

He spun the date wheels back through the months, years and centuries, until they landed on 5th September 1270. He felt the pressure of Maya's hand on his arm, and he pressed "Go".

Everything around them faded to a deep, swirling grey. When the mist cleared they found themselves gazing on a very changed scene....

Chapter 2

Discovered!

The rough, moss-covered walls had become smooth and glossy and hung with tapestries. The sky had disappeared, replaced by a steeply pitched, hammerbeam roof. The long grass underfoot had become a polished stone floor. The room glowed cosily in the light of wall-mounted tallow candles.

Two men were standing on the far side of the room near a blazing hearth. One was a big, bearded man with a tartan cloak and a sword in his belt. The other had a smooth face with a long, sharp nose. He wore a green belted tunic, yellow leggings and pointy shoes. Fortunately for Joe and Maya, the men were deep in conversation and failed to see the children emerge out of thin air.

Joe reacted quickest, tugging Maya behind a nearby tapestry, just as the bigger man looked up.

"What's wrong, Constable?" they heard the other one say.

"Nothin', Sir Archibald," came the reply. "Perhaps a gust o' wind from the chimney caused yon tapestry to stir… As you see, there's little that escapes ma eagle eye."

"Except for the theft of the chalice," said Sir Archibald tetchily. He had a thin, reedy voice that contrasted with the constable's deeper tones.

"Och, but I caught that no-good lady-in-waiting, Joanna, right enough," said the constable. "She took that chalice, sir, ah'm sure of it. And ah'll torture her till she tells me where it is."

Joe and Maya stood as straight and still as they could behind the heavy woollen tapestry. In the half-light, Joe could see that his clothing had transformed. He was now wearing a short tunic with leggings, and a large hood that covered his head, neck and shoulders. Maya's jeans and t-shirt had been replaced by a long, loose-fitting, belted gown with tight sleeves. The smells of dusty fabric and woodsmoke tickled Joe's nose and he felt as if he might sneeze. He pinched his nostrils hard.

Sir Archibald was saying: "Well, constable, just make sure the chalice is returned to the chapel by nightfall. Everyone's talking about this wretched curse. As steward of this castle, it's causing me no end of worry. A laundry maid, an undercook and a kitchen maid have already deserted. Rumour has it that some of our finest knights have even been seen slipping away."

The sneeze was coming. There was nothing Joe could do about it. His nose and throat were itching like mad from the dust.

"Ah'm all too aware of the problem, sir," replied the constable. "Ah've had a guardsman disappear on me, and Sir William has lost his squire. What with these reports of the Earl of Athelbane marchin' towards us, things can only get worse."

"*Aaah… aaah…*" Joe couldn't stop the sounds escaping his throat. He clamped a hand over his mouth, and Maya shoved her own hand over his for good measure. But it was like trying to plug a volcano.

"*Ah-choooo!!!*" the sneeze erupted.

They stared at each other in horror. A second later, the tapestry was pulled roughly aside and they cringed before an enraged constable.

"Who the devil are you?" he bellowed at them, raising his sword high above his head. "Speak now or ah'll slice the pair o' ye in twain."

"I–I…" stammered Joe.

"We saw some servants running away from your castle," said Maya, her eyes travelling fearfully up the length of the steel blade now poised above her head.

"We thought you might need some replacements," added Joe.

The sword trembled in the constable's hand. "D'you believe 'em, Sir Archibald? Or shall ah run 'em through?"

After a moment's contemplation, the steward glided across the floor as smoothly as if he were on castors. "Sheathe your sword, constable," he said in honeyed tones. "I doubt Athelbane would employ such an incompetent young pair as spies, and if they *had* stolen the chalice, they'd hardly still be here lurking behind tapestries, would they? No, I expect they're what they say they are: a pair of locals from the village seeking employment."

He smiled at Maya, which was somehow far more scary than the constable's rage. "You, girl. Think you can be a lady's maid?"

Without waiting for an answer, his attention flicked to Joe. "And you laddie, how would you like to be squire to Sir William?"

* * *

Before they knew it, Joe and Maya had been hired. The steward left Joe with the constable while he escorted Maya to her duties. Five minutes later, he returned for Joe. He ushered him out of the room and into the great hall. A fire burned in the giant hearth, reflecting in the gleaming armour and weapons lining the walls.

Joe's eye was caught by a movement. He turned in time to see a black-cloaked figure walking quickly away from the door. It appeared that Joe and Maya hadn't been the only ones eavesdropping on the constable and steward! As the figure hurried down a passage at the far end, something fell from a fold in the cloak. It looked like a string of beads.

Joe felt a strong urge to investigate, but the constable jabbed him in the back. "What are you doin' laddie? Get after Sir Archibald if you dunnae want to feel the sharp end o' mah sword!"

Joe scurried after the steward, who led him into a dimly lit turret and up a spiral stone staircase. They arrived at an upper-floor corridor. Sir Archibald opened a door off the corridor and steered Joe into a spacious room dominated by a grand four-poster bed. "This is Sir William's bedchamber. He's meeting with his father, Lord Robert, just now. I will inform him of your appointment. Now you wait here. If I catch you wandering about the castle, I'll set the constable onto you."

Left alone, Joe debated what to do. Despite the steward's warning, he really wanted to go downstairs and check out that object dropped by the mysterious eavesdropper. He was on the point of creeping back to the great hall when he heard the sound of faint voices talking. Joe turned. The voices seemed to be coming from behind a heavy door opposite the bed.

Joe crept over to the door. He knelt and put his eye to the keyhole. There was another room there, decorated with shields and tapestries. He could see part of a young man, wearing dark red leggings and a green embroidered tunic. Joe couldn't see who he was talking to, but by placing his ear to the keyhole, he could just about hear what they were saying.

"You stole it, sir, admit it!" said the young man.

"Nonsense!" cried the other, also young and male. "You are without question the thief. Your motive is far stronger than mine."

Their voices faded as the men headed down a corridor on the far side of the room.

Had they stolen the chalice? Joe wondered. And what about the eavesdropper downstairs? There was no sign of Sir William. Would he have time to follow the young men, or should he head downstairs and see what it was the mysterious figure had dropped?

Chapter 3

The Holy Chalice

Joe made up his mind. He would risk the wrath of the steward and his constable. He'd head downstairs and check out the clue left by the eavesdropper. After making sure there was no sound in the passageway outside, he slipped out of the room and made his way to the spiral staircase.

He was halfway down the dark, narrow stairwell when he heard footsteps beneath him coming up the stairs.

Joe panicked. If it was the steward, he was done for!

Joe was scrambling back up the stairs when he was stayed by a whispered voice.

"Joe, it's okay. It's me!"

He nearly cried out with relief. It was Maya.

They both returned to the bottom of the stairs, and quickly told each other about their new jobs. Maya was working for a tall, rather beautiful lady called Lady Ada Hamilton, the widowed sister of Lord Robert Mackenzie. She had dispatched Maya with a message for her son, Sir James Hamilton.

"You can deliver it afterwards," said Joe. "First, I want you to help me find something." He told her about the eavesdropper and the beads. Maya, of course, was eager to join him in the hunt.

They sneaked into the great hall. The string of beads was still there, by the entrance to a passage. Maya examined them. "They look like those rosary beads that Catholic nuns and priests wear," she said.

"Well, whoever dropped them went this way," said Joe, heading down the passageway. It led to a small, simple room – a chapel, to judge from the furnishings. There were oak pews and, at the far end, an altar, lit by candles. Kneeling at the altar was the same black-cloaked figure Joe had seen eavesdropping.

The praying figure whirled around as they entered. He had a gaunt face and a small, carefully groomed beard. When he saw Joe and Maya, his fearful expression turned to indignation. "You dare to disturb the castle chaplain at his prayers! What do you want?"

Maya's next words shocked both the chaplain and Joe. "The constable," she said, "has ordered us to find out what you were doing listening at the door of the steward's room."

It was a brazen lie, but she spoke it with real conviction. Joe couldn't help being impressed.

"We know it was you," Maya continued, "because you dropped these."

She handed the chaplain his rosary beads. He stared at them guiltily, then looked up at her. "I was afeared," he said. "We're all afeared right now. It was wrong of me to eavesdrop, but I was desperate for news about the missing chalice."

He looked around miserably, until his eyes fixed on a gold container, resting on a marble plinth next to the altar. Easily the most beautiful object in the chapel, it looked like a miniature cathedral entrance made entirely of gold. It had a pair of arched doors, a trumpeting angel carved into each one. The doors stood open, showing an empty, velvet-lined interior.

"The chalice was always kept locked in this reliquary," said the chaplain. "I was visiting Lord Robert in his chambers this morning, trying to persuade him not to neglect his prayers and to attend mass more regularly. You can imagine my shock when, upon my return, I found the reliquary open and the chalice gone!

This, don't forget, is the Holy Chalice of St Ninian. Since time immemorial, it's belonged to the Mackenzies of Cranston. Of course, the ancient legend talks of the good fortune that the chalice has bestowed on Castle Cranston. If the chalice were ever to be lost, Castle Cranston will fall. And this has been confirmed by a recent, startling discovery. Here, let me show you…"

The chaplain opened a small jewelled box and pulled out a black scroll, unfurled it and showed it to Maya and Joe. On the black parchment the following words were written in gold ink in a flowing calligraphy with lots of curls and swirls:

If this chalice e'er be taken
From within these walls
The Mackenzies be forsaken
Castle Cranston falls

The chaplain's eyes grew dark and seemed to glitter with a fearful kind of awe. "This I believe was a warning from God," he declared. "Lord Robert is not the pious man his father was. He has fallen into heathen ways. Make no mistake, the loss of the chalice is God's punishment!"

"Right," said Joe, raising his eyebrows at Maya. "So who has keys to the reli… the reliq… the gold box?"

"Myself, the steward and Lord Robert have the only keys," said the chaplain. He showed them his, hanging from a belt around his waist. "I had this with me on my visit to Lord Robert."

"And did Lord Robert have his key?" asked Maya.

"Aye, he had it where he always does: hanging on a chain around his neck, where he should be wearing a crucifix, of course!" he muttered darkly.

"Which leaves the steward's key?" said Maya, swapping a glance with Joe. *The steward! But what possible motive would he have to steal the chalice?*

They all turned at a sound behind them. There *was* the steward, lurking in the chapel entrance. "You two should not be in here," he said. His voice was quiet, but coated with ice. "Why aren't you at your duties? I ought to set the constable on to you."

Maya opened her mouth to reply, but the steward cut in: "But, never mind that! Lord Robert has announced there will be a feast tonight. You two are needed in the kitchen, immediately. Every spare pair of hands is required to help with the preparations."

"A feast?" queried the chaplain. "Surely this is no time to be…."

"On the contrary," replied the steward in his oily tone. We shall make merry tonight, and banish the gloom that seems to have infected this castle. And there shall be no more talk of curses, Father Dalliel. Do you understand me?"

At this, the chaplain fell silent.

Joe wondered how long the steward had been listening at the door. Did he know they'd been discussing the keys? He was about to follow Maya and the steward out of the chapel when his eye was caught by something hanging from the base of a wrought-iron candle-holder next to the marble plinth. Peering closer, he saw that it was a twist of green and gold thread. He quickly snatched it up and pocketed it, before scurrying after Maya.

"The kitchen is that way," said the steward, pointing down another passageway leading off the great hall. Then he grabbed Joe by the shoulder and swung him around to face him. A long, bony finger pointed into Joe's face. "I heard you questioning the chaplain about some keys," the steward whispered menacingly. "People who ask questions don't last long around here. Remember, Athelbane will be here very soon. If you carry on this way, I'll put you two atop the battlements to give his bowmen target practice. Now be off with you!"

Joe and Maya, still breathing hard after this encounter, entered the big, crowded kitchen, hot with greasy cooking smells. It was dominated by a giant hearth, where a suckling pig was being roasted on a spit and a bubbling iron cauldron hung over the flames. There were servants everywhere, fetching wood for the fire, turning the spit, stirring soup, rolling pastry, chopping vegetables, plucking birds and gutting fish.

The only person who didn't seem to belong was a well-dressed young man with a pale, twitchy face and black, curly hair, loitering by a shelf containing a row of pottery jars. Joe recognized his dark red leggings and green embroidered tunic. This was the same man he'd overheard in Sir William's bedchamber. He wondered what he was doing down here in the kitchen.

The young noble didn't look too pleased at being stared at and quickly departed the room.

A moment later, the cook – a lady of large build – came bustling into the kitchen. She was wearing a white headdress and matching apron and was carrying a heavy-looking book. "Sir James, I've found that recipe for cockatrice," she said, looking expectantly towards the spot where the young man had been. Her face fell when she saw he had gone. She turned to Maya and Joe. "Did you see Sir James just now?"

"That was Sir James Hamilton?" said Maya. "My Lady Hamilton's son?"

"Why of course it was, lassie," laughed the cook. "Such an honour to receive a personal visit from a member of the earl's family. And he seemed so interested to know if we could make cockatrice. And now he's gone. How disappointing!"

"I have a message for him," said Maya, heading for the door.

The steward, just arriving, snatched the note from her fingers. "I'll take that, thank you," he said. "Cook, these two are here to help with the feast. Keep an eye on them will you. They have a tendency to wander!"

Chapter 4

A Fateful Feast

For Joe and Maya, the rest of the afternoon passed in a blur of activity as they joined the army of servants preparing the eight-course banquet. They gathered herbs from the garden behind the kitchen, stirred the stew, carried loaves from the bakery and barrels of ale from the cellars. The steward, in his sinister way, seemed to be everywhere, keeping a constant watch on them and making sure they never got even a moment to themselves.

As the sun sank beneath the hills and the sky dimmed, torches were lit, giving the castle a festive glow. Minstrels dressed in colourful costumes appeared in the gallery overlooking the great hall and played uplifting tunes on lute, bagpipes and drums. The earl's family began to gather and take their seats at the table. Joe and Maya were among those serving up the courses, and they were warned by the steward to pay special attention to the needs of their master and mistress.

Lord Robert Mackenzie, head of the household, seemed to Joe a dour, grim-faced man, with eyes the colour of storm clouds, sunken cheeks and down-turned mouth half hidden by his frosty grey beard. If he'd arranged the feast to try and cheer himself up, it clearly hadn't worked.

"Eat, drink and be merry!" he ordered his guests gloomily, "for the chalice is gone, Athelbane is on the march, and soon we'll all be dead!"

"Don't be so quick to lose hope, my lord," laughed his son, Sir William, a big, handsome, rosy-cheeked man. "I for one do not believe in this curse. It's nothing more than a stale legend – a mere story – given a new lease of life by that mysterious black parchment that turned up a few weeks ago in the …."

"The curse is real!" declared the chaplain from the far end of the table. "The black parchment is a warning from God. To say otherwise is a sin."

Sir William smiled. "Why, come Father Dalliel, I never took you for a superstitious man. Do you not think it rather curious that this warning should suddenly appear out of nowhere, and then the chalice is mysteriously stolen? It's almost as if the two events are connected in some way."

"Blasphemy!" muttered the chaplain.

Sir William ignored him. "If you ask me, it's all a plot to bring down our family. It won't work, though, for I hope the chalice will soon be recovered and the thief brought to justice. Constable, how goes the investigation?"

"Very well, sir!" bellowed the constable, who was standing to attention nearby. "Ah'm well on ma way to extractin' a confession from the young woman, Joanna."

"And just what evidence do you have against this trusted member of the household, constable?" asked Lord Robert.

"Och, there's no doubt it was her, m'lord. She was seen comin' out o' the chapel at the time the chalice was taken. The greedy lass was clearly plannin' tae sell it tae one o' the local monasteries. These holy relics fetch very high prices, so ahm told, m'lord."

"Well…perhaps," said Sir William, sounding entirely unconvinced. "The timing of the theft seems very suspicious, as I've said." He cast a long glance at the steward, who was loitering nearby. "For all we know, Athelbane may have paid someone to steal it just to damage our morale – soften us up before his siege…. I would widen your investigation, constable. Athelbane would not have trusted a girl like Joanna to do his bidding. He would have enlisted someone more senior…." He turned to Joe. "Well, well, enough of all this, we are here to dine. Young squire, bring me some of my favourite, will you?"

"Your favourite?"

"Aye! Lamprey in vinegar! Cook always sets some aside for me because she knows how much I love it. Go fetch me some, lad."

In the kitchen, Joe repeated the request to the cook, who laughed and took down a jar from the shelf. Joe noticed that it was exactly where Sir James had been lurking suspiciously earlier. "Sir William loves his lampreys," she chuckled as she poured some of the grey pickled eel-like fish into a bowl. "He can never resist them at a feast!"

Back in the great hall, Maya was refilling Lady Hamilton's wine goblet when her son Sir James leaned close and whispered. "Mother, I've decided that I will go on crusade after all. … The Saracens are attacking our Christian brethren in the Holy Land, and the king of France is calling for volunteers."

Lady Hamilton looked alarmed by this news. "Please don't go," she pleaded. "I lost my husband, your father, to the crusades. I don't want to lose you as well."

"My mind is made up, mother."

Maya's ears pricked up at Lady Hamilton's reply: "But you told me you wouldn't go unless you had the chalice with you to bring you luck."

"That was before this black parchment was discovered," her son went on. "I realized then that I could never take the chalice with me. I'll go without it. Fear not, all will be well. I'll leave tomorrow. The sooner I am away from here the better."

* * *

When the feast was over, and they were clearing the remains from the table, Maya reported this conversation to Joe. "I think

Sir James stole the chalice," she said. "He obviously wanted to take it on crusade with him."

"I'm not sure," said Joe. "Did you see the way Sir William was looking at the steward when he suggested Athelbane had paid someone to steal it? I think the steward is probably our thief. After all, he has the key for that relic box thing."

"We shouldn't forget Joanna," Maya reminded him. "She was virtually caught red-handed, according the constable." She looked around her. They were, for now at least, alone in the great hall. "Why don't we go and see her now – see if we think she's guilty or not?" she suggested.

"What about the steward?" said Joe, looking nervously over his shoulder.

"He went into his room. This may be our only chance."

"Right, well they said Joanna was in the dungeon," Joe said.

After a quick search, they found, in an alcove near the hearth, a set of steps heading downwards.

"This must be it," said Maya.

The stairwell was narrow, the stones black with age. As they descended, a chill and dampness seeped into their bones, making them shiver. It seemed they were entering a place of no return.

At the bottom of the steps was a heavy wooden door with iron studs and a small barred window. In front of the door, on a little stool, slumped the jailer. He was dozing, an empty flagon of ale by his feet.

"We're in luck," murmured Maya. "The jailer's asleep. I can see the key on that ring attached to his belt. We'll be able to get in and speak to her."

Just then, they heard a terrible, gut-wrenching roar from upstairs. It sounded like someone in mortal pain.

"Help!" wailed a female voice. "Sir William is ailing!"

A terrible thought struck Joe then. Had Sir William been poisoned? He remembered Sir James in the kitchen earlier. Had he or the steward poisoned the lamprey? Sir William had suspected a plot, and now maybe someone was trying to silence him. He had to get to him, and fast.

Chapter 5

Joanna's Tale

Maya could see that Joe looked torn. "It's alright," she whispered. "You go and check on Sir William and I'll talk to Joanna."

Joe glanced nervously at the slumbering jailer. "Are you sure you'll be okay?"

"Uh, I think I can cope without you, cuz," she smiled.

"Be careful, yeah? Don't wake him up. You don't want to end up imprisoned down here."

"Don't worry. I'll be as quiet as a mouse," she assured him, rolling her eyes.

As Joe scampered back up the dungeon steps, Maya crept quietly towards the jailer. She was reaching for the ring of keys on his belt when he suddenly bellowed, "Get off me yer great...."

Maya leapt back in fright, then relaxed as she realized he was just talking in his sleep. When his breathing had become regular again, she began, very gently, grappling with the clasp on the iron ring. It was stiff and fiddly. Finally, after tearing a thumbnail, she managed to open it. Heart thumping, she slowly slid the ring off his belt. She had just removed it when the jailer shifted on his stool. Maya froze.

He muttered to himself again, but didn't open his eyes. After waiting a few moments, she moved towards the cell door. There were three keys on the ring. The second one fitted. The key made a loud clink as it turned, but this time the jailer didn't stir.

Maya pushed open the heavy door, and heard a soft gasp from the shadows.

"Please, no more beatings," a girl's voice begged.

"It's alright," whispered Maya, closing the door behind her. "I'm not going to hurt you."

In the dim light filtering through the door's barred window, she caught a flash of red hair.

"Who are you?" asked the voice. "What do you want with me?"

She could see the girl's outline huddled on a dirty straw mattress in the corner. "You're Joanna, right?"

"I am." The girl peered at her with wide, frightened eyes. "You look like a servant," she murmured. "How did you get in here?"

Maya jangled the keys. "Sneaked past the jailer."

"You'll be in trouble if he wakes," whispered the girl. "Who are you anyway?"

"I'm a lady-in-waiting, like you, working for Lady Hamilton."

"They've replaced me already then," sniffed the girl. "That means I'm done for."

"Not necessarily," said Maya, seating herself by Joanna's side. "If you really are innocent, I might be able to help you clear your name. But you have to tell me the truth."

"I keep telling the constable, I wasn't anywhere near the chapel this morning when the chalice was stolen."

Her pale, grubby face moved briefly into the light, and Maya could see she'd been crying.

"Where were you then?" Maya asked.

"I was in the kitchen, giving cook instructions from Lady Hamilton about luncheon. The chaplain said the clock had just struck nine when he returned to the chapel to find the chalice missing. He said he saw me leaving as he arrived. But I remember being in the kitchen talking to cook when the bell was ringing for nine."

"Can't cook back you up?"

"She tried, but the constable thinks I must have gone straight from the kitchen to the chapel."

"What exactly did the chaplain say he saw?"

"Said he saw a girl with red hair just like mine, and dressed like me, too. But he only saw her from behind. Then he went into the chapel and saw the reliquary box open and the chalice gone."

Maya frowned. "Sounds to me as if someone disguised themselves as you."

"Or else the chaplain lied," said Joanna.

"Why would he do that?"

"Maybe because *he* stole the chalice."

"The chaplain?" gasped Maya.

Joanna nodded. "He's always saying that he despairs of Lord Robert for his unchristian ways. He says God will punish him. What better way of making that happen than by stealing the chalice and bringing down that ancient curse upon the House of Mackenzie? He probably sees himself as God's agent."

Maya took the girl's cool hand. "I can't believe they're blaming you for this. I'm going to try and help you."

There was a clattering sound outside. "Eh? Wha's goin' on?" the jailer's voice thundered. "Where are mah keys???!!!"

Chapter 6

God's Punishment

When he reached the upstairs corridor, Joe found Sir William collapsed there, surrounded by Lord Robert, the chaplain, the steward and several servants.

"I'm his squire," said Joe. "Let me through!" He helped a very pale Sir William to his feet and supported him as he staggered into his chamber and fell on the bed. With no one else in earshot he took the opportunity to voice his concerns. Bending close to Sir William, he whispered: "Sire, I saw your cousin,

Sir James, acting suspiciously in the kitchen earlier. I think he may have poisoned you."

Sir William's eyes widened on hearing this. He stared at Joe in shock, or, perhaps, disbelief.

Just then, the others arrived in the room.

"It looks grave to me," groaned Lord Robert.

"The physician is coming," said the steward.

"I will pray for him," said the chaplain solemnly, but his true feelings were obvious from the smirk on his face: *this was God's punishment for blasphemy.*

The castle physician, wearing a red gown and white cap, arrived a few minutes later.

"I need privacy," he immediately announced. "Everyone please leave!"

Lord Robert and the chaplain departed, and the steward ordered out the servants.

But as Joe was leaving, Sir William clutched his arm. "I want my squire here," he croaked. "I trust him."

"Very well, he can stay," said the physician. "I may need an assistant."

The steward gritted his teeth, but nodded and left the room.

Joe held Sir William still as the physician took out his knife and opened cuts in his skin. "To let out the bad blood," he explained.

It made no difference. Sir William suffered and sweated. "My tongue… I can't feel it," he mumbled. "So dizzy...." Then he vomited into a bowl. The calm that followed this was brief. Within minutes, he was screaming in agony, twisting and turning and rubbing madly at his skin. "Ants!" he cried. "Ants all over my body! Get them off me!"

Joe mopped the sick man's brow with a cool, damp cloth. At length, Sir William grew quieter, the screams giving way to groans and mutterings. "James," he rasped. "James, why do you hate me so?"

Finally, he fell asleep.

"He is peaceful for now," said the physician. "Go to the library, lad, and fetch me my *Herbal*."

"Your *Herbal*?"

"Aye, the big, black book containing descriptions of poisonous and medicinal plants. You'll find it in the second alcove on the right. Be quick about it, laddie. We haven't much time."

Joe remembered catching a glimpse of a room full of books near the chapel. He headed there.

There were no torches burning on the library walls because of the danger of fire, so Joe stole a candle from the chapel to light his way. The library was a gloomy, musty-smelling place occupying the lower part of one of the castle's turrets. This gave it a circular shape, with shelf upon shelf of books surrounding him on all sides. Hundreds of ancient tomes were squeezed on to the cramped shelves, and a twisting stairway led to an upper tier of yet more books – paradise for a book worm like Joe, except he doubted he'd find any detective stories here. Staring down at him from the upper-tier balcony was a fierce-looking statue of a bearded man, a heavy sword in his clasped hands. Joe noted a similarity with Lord Robert and wondered if it was one of his ancestors.

He held the candle up to the cracked, ancient spines and tried to decipher the gold-leaf words. In the second alcove, he found one inscribed "*De Vegetabilibus* Albertus Magnus". Joe guessed this might be what he was looking for.

He lugged the heavy volume to a table in the middle of the room and began leafing through the creamy yellow pages. They were filled with beautiful hand-writing and colourful illusions of plants and flowers. He knew the physician wanted him to return quickly with the book, but Joe couldn't resist checking it out himself. He just wanted to see if his suspicion that Sir William had been poisoned was correct. He'd witnessed the symptoms – it shouldn't be that hard to find the plant responsible and then read what it said about a cure.

The book was written in Latin, but Joe was able to recognise a few of the words, having received some lessons in the language from his granddad. He was getting engrossed in the book when he was startled by a scraping noise above his head, like the scuffing of a shoe. He looked up. *Was someone else there?* Raising his candle, he scanned the circular balcony but could see nothing up there except books and shadows – and the statue of course. Its ferocious eyes seemed to bore into him as if accusing him of some evil deed.

"You didn't make that noise, did you?" Joe smiled.

The statue didn't reply.

Must have been a rat, Joe thought as he sat back down and tried to concentrate on the book.

A few minutes later, he heard the noise again. It was like a shifting of feet. He jerked his head up and got quite a shock: the statue seemed to have moved!

Chapter 7

Poisoned!

Maya tried to make herself as small as possible as the jailer came storming into the cell. His lantern shook in his hand, sending shadows dancing over the walls.

"Wha's goin' on?" he bellowed at Joanna. "Why is this door open, and what are mah keys doin' in here?"

"What?" answered Joanna blearily as if she'd just woken from sleep.

"Is someone else in here?" growled the jailer, swinging the lantern wildly to try and see into every corner.

Maya shrank from its light, burying herself deeper into the gap between the straw mattress and the wall. Only Joanna's body was shielding her from exposure.

"Why, don't you remember, sir?" said Joanna, sounding more wakeful now. "While you were drinking earlier, you opened the door and kindly invited me to join you for an ale. When I declined, you promptly fell asleep."

"Nonsense! I would never do such a thing!" frowned the jailer, staring ever more intensely at a shadow behind Joanna.

"You were drunk, sir!" laughed the lady-in-waiting, raising herself slightly to cover the shadow. "I'm sure you won't do it again. And I promise I won't tell the constable of this incident if you will do something for me now."

The jailer, looking sheepish, asked what she wanted.

"See over there," she said, pointing to some writing carved into the wall. "It offends me to see such a word on the wall of my cell. Could you please remove it."

While the jailer was peering at the graffiti, Maya took her cue and dashed quickly from the cell. As she bounded up the dungeon steps, she heard the jailer's puzzled response: "But all it says is *Fraser*."

"Exactly," said Joanna. "I've never cared for that name."

* * *

Joe was sure the statue was now closer to the edge of the balcony than it had been before. He stared at it for a full minute, but it didn't move again. He rubbed his eyes and yawned. It was late. He was tired.

He must have imagined it.

He returned his attention to the book, trying hard to remember some of the Latin his grandfather had taught him. Then his attention was caught by some words:

Lingua torporis. Nausea. Vomitus. Frigus, lentum pellem.

Some of them he recognised: nausea; vomiting; cold skin? There were more words after that, which he couldn't understand. Next to them was an illustration of a horror-struck man with ants crawling on him. He recalled Sir William's agonised cry: *Ants all over my body! Get them off me!*

This must be it!

He looked at the plant illustrated on that page, and gasped. The plant, called monkshood, had dark green leaves and sinister purple drooping flowers that he immediately recognised: he'd seen them through a window that very day, growing in a shady corner of the castle's kitchen garden.

So Sir William *had* been poisoned!

Joe quickly read up on the antidote. The Herbal recommended small doses of digitalis and atropine. Hopefully the physician would know where to get those. He closed the book and was about to return it to the shelf when a deep grinding sound from above made him freeze. Too petrified to move, Joe could only swivel his eyes heavenwards. What he saw filled him with horror. The statue, now positioned directly over his head, was toppling off the balcony and plunging straight towards him!

* * *

Maya was standing in the empty castle kitchen. It was very late now and everyone had gone to bed. The only illumination was moonlight streaming in through the door to the garden. Counting the seconds in her head, she began walking at a reasonable pace out through the door, along the passageway, across the great hall and down the corridor that led to the chapel. She stopped at the chapel entrance. It had taken her two minutes to reach here.

Checking to make sure no one was about, she proceeded up the aisle and stood before the opened reliquary, still counting in her head. After miming opening the box and removing the chalice, she returned to the passage outside. A little more than three minutes had elapsed since she'd left the kitchen.

"Excuse me! Can I help you?"

Maya spun around as the sharp voice rang out.

The chaplain was glaring at her from the doorway of a room to the side of the altar.

She stared right back, while fighting to get her breathing under control. "Father Dalliel. I'm glad you're here, er, I have a question for you."

"What is it?"

"You said you saw Joanna coming out of the chapel just after nine o'clock. Is that right?"

"Aye."

"How long after exactly?"

"What is this? Why are you asking?"

"I'm… I'm helping the constable… with his investigations."

The chaplain thought for a moment. "It was no more than a minute," he said. "The bell was striking nine when I left Lord Robert's room."

"Then you couldn't have seen her," said Maya firmly.

The chaplain scowled. "Are you accusing *me*, a man of the cloth, of lying?"

"No…. Well, maybe. I mean I know how much you wanted God to punish Lord Robert. Perhaps you…."

His eyes widened with indignation. "Now you're saying *I* stole the chalice! How dare you!"

Maya put up her hands soothingly as he began striding towards her. "Father, please," she said. "I'm not saying you definitely stole the chalice. All I know is that an innocent girl is stuck down there in the dungeon and only you can save her. Speak to the constable. Tell him you may have been mistaken. I've just timed the walk from the kitchen and there's no way she could have done it in under three minutes."

* * *

Joe leapt to one side just as the statue came crashing down, smashing the chair where he'd been sitting. It shattered on impact, sending chunks of stone flying in all directions. He cried out as a sharp piece of stone sliced through the skin of his leg. The candle snuffed out.

Joe lay on the floor in darkness, covered in dust and splinters. Breathing hard, his heart battering his ribs, he tried very hard not to panic. *What was happening?* He couldn't form thoughts – couldn't think what to do. Too scared.

Something was coming towards him – coming very slowly down the stairs from the balcony. He could hear its footsteps creaking as they came closer.

Joe almost sobbed with fear. Seeing a glimmer of light from the passage outside, he began slithering towards it, kicking aside pieces of broken chair as he staggered frantically to his feet. Pain lanced through his leg as he put weight on it, but he didn't care. All he cared about was getting away from whatever was coming after him. He spun out of the library and hobbled down the passage. The chapel to his left seemed to offer a chance of safety. He crouched in the shadows just inside the entrance, listening, but all he could hear was the steam engine sounds of his own breath.

Then he caught the echo of footsteps coming down the passage. He pressed himself deeper into the shadows, squeezing his eyes shut and praying.

The footsteps passed on without pausing.

Joe counted slowly to fifty, then crept from his hiding place. He limped across the darkened great hall towards the staircase that would return him to Sir William's bedchamber. But before he got halfway up the stairs, someone grabbed him.

Chapter 8

Night Terror!

Joe went rigid with terror as the hand locked around his arm. He tried frantically to break free while his mind spun with horrid thoughts. *The killer had got him! His life was over!* He writhed and twisted but the iron grip was impossible to shake off. His captor forced him to turn around, and Joe nearly lost his footing in the narrow stairwell. As he was pushed down hard against the steps, a stab of pain shot through his injured leg. A bright light flared in his face. A figure loomed above him. Joe immediately recognized the pale, twitching face with its small beard.

Lady Hamilton's son, Sir James!

The young noble brought the torch he was carrying close to Joe's face – so close he could feel its heat start to scorch his skin. "What are you doing creeping about, boy?" Sir James growled under his breath. "I ought to kill you right now." The flame was almost licking Joe's cheek. He could feel droplets of sweat breaking out on his face. Sir James whispered: "I can guess why you're here you little snake. Just remember: I've got my eye on you. If you do anything to cross me, you're dead."

"Alright, alright!" gasped Joe. "I understand."

The flame moved away, and Sir James released his grip. He stood up, and Joe caught a glimpse of a tunic over chain mail. The tunic was blue with a gold lion in its centre. Then the knight turned. With a sweep of his cloak and a clatter of iron-soled boots, he was gone.

It was a long time before Joe felt calm enough to continue his way to Sir William's bedchamber. The physician greeted him at the door.

"Where have you been?" he demanded. "Where's the Herbal I asked you to fetch?"

"There… there was an accident," explained Joe, wiping the sweat from his face.

"An accident?" gasped the physician.

"Yes, but that doesn't matter now. What matters is that Sir William has been poisoned. I looked it up myself. The poison was extracted from monkshood."

"Poisoned? Are you sure? But who would do such a thing?"

Joe was tempted to tell the physician everything, but then Sir James's words echoed through his head and he lost his nerve.

"I don't know," he muttered, suddenly feeling exhausted. "The Herbal suggested digitalis and... and… atro… something."

"Atropine? Aye, that sounds right." The physician studied Joe, whose eyes were drooping. "You'd better get to bed, laddie. You've done well, thank you. I'll take over from here. We'll speak again in the morning."

* * *

Joe bathed and bandaged his leg as best he could, flopped on to his narrow bed in the corner of Sir William's room and fell into a deep sleep. He was woken the following morning by a shaft of misty sunlight that fell through the arched window above him. The physician was dozing in a chair by the giant four-poster bed. Sir William lay there so wan and still, Joe feared he might have died during the night.

The physician awoke as Joe approached. "Your master is doing well," he smiled, to Joe's relief. "He's sleeping peacefully. Go fetch some fresh water and a little bread and cheese. We'll see if he has an appetite."

As Joe was limping along the upstairs passageway, he was pleased to see Maya emerge from Lady Hamilton's room.

"Hey cuz!" she cried excitedly. "I've got so much to tell you."

"Me too," smiled Joe.

"What have you done to your leg?" she asked.

"I'll tell you…." Joe replied.

As they headed down the steps and across the great hall, they told each other their stories. Maya listened wide-eyed to

Joe's terrifying experience in the library and the stairwell.

"Sir James has to be the poisoner," she said emphatically when Joe had finished. "And it must have been him who tried to squash you with that statue in the library to stop you finding the antidote to the poison."

Joe nodded. "I think you're right, but Joanna seems to suspect that the chaplain stole the chalice… that's interesting."

"I wish I could have got him to confess," sighed Maya. "Or even to admit that Joanna might not be the thief. It looks as if the poor girl is doomed to spend the rest of her days in that horrid dungeon…. Hmm. I wonder if Sir James and the chaplain are working together." Then a thought struck her. "Hey, why don't we check out the library – see if we can find any clues?"

"But I have to–" Joe began.

"It'll only take a few minutes. Come on!"

Joe would have preferred never to set foot in that room again, but Maya was right: they ought to search it now before the mess got cleaned up. After checking to make sure no one was around, he hobbled after her. When they reached the library, he gasped.

"Are you sure you didn't dream it all, cuz?" asked Maya.

Joe wandered into the room, his jaw slack with amazement. The place was perfectly tidy, with not a trace of broken statue anywhere. The Herbal was back on its shelf. He looked up at the balcony.

"The statue was up there," he said, pointing. "Someone – Sir James, I suppose – must have cleaned the place up last night. I swear I didn't dream it."

"Well there's one way to check," said Maya, mounting the steps to the balcony. "Perhaps there's…." Then she gave a whoop of triumph.

"What?" called Joe.

"I can see the mark in the dust where the statue must have stood. And there are drag marks. It was obviously pushed to a position above the table where you were sitting. So you weren't dreaming after all."

"Told you!" said Joe, hobbling up the steps to join her. He found her crouching to look at something else near the drag marks.

"What is it?" he asked.

"Looks like a footprint," she said, then glanced up, frowning. "Does Sir James have very small feet, by any chance?"

Joe had to agree the footprint was on the small side. He put his own foot next to it for comparison. It was even smaller than his. Taking out his smartphone, he took a photo of the footprint with his foot next to it.

"Next time I see Sir James, I shall take a close look at his feet," said Joe.

To his surprise, Maya giggled. She put a hand to her mouth as he glared at her. "Sorry, cuz, but what you just said sounded so funny, especially with that serious look on your face."

"You two!" They were startled by the harsh shout from below. The steward glared up at them. "What are you doing up there? Get back to your duties at once!"

His suspicious gaze never left them as they hurried down the stairs and out of the library.

"I swear that man has some medieval form of radar in his head," whispered Maya as they made their way down the corridor. "How come he always knows exactly where we are?"

* * *

A little while later, Lady Hamilton was dictating a letter to Maya in her boudoir, when there was a sharp knock on the door.

"Come in," called Lady Hamilton.

The steward entered. "My lady," he said, "I have bad tidings."

Her hand rose to her cheek. "Is it Sir William?" she asked.

"No, ma'am, he is doing well, praise God. No, this news concerns your son."

Lady Hamilton paled. "James? What about him?"

"He's gone, my lady. He departed the castle on horseback an hour ago. He left no message."

Lady Hamilton groped for the chair behind her and sat down heavily. "He told me last night he was going on crusade," she said weakly. "I had hoped there would be time to dissuade him from this folly." She looked up at the steward. "Dispatch a search party to find him and bring him back."

"B-but, my lady," stuttered the steward. "We are preparing for a siege. We need all hands–"

"Fetch my son!" ordered Lady Hamilton sternly.

"Yes… yes, of course, my lady," Sir Archbald replied, with a small bow of the head.

The steward departed.

* * *

Maya caught up with Joe in the servants' hall behind the kitchen where they gathered for lunch. They seated themselves at the end of the table, as far from the steward's unnerving presence as they could get.

"Do you think Sir James really went on crusade?" Maya whispered to Joe.

He shook his head. "I think he's gone to join Athelbane."

Maya stared at him, waiting for him to go on.

"He's obviously decided that Athelbane will be victorious in the coming battle and he wants to make sure he's on the winning side. He still thinks he's managed to kill Sir William, remember? I'll bet he hopes that'll impress Athelbane enough to let him join his forces. Or perhaps he's been working for the enemy all along."

"Sounds possible," muttered Maya. "But if so, his mother knows nothing about it."

"I wouldn't be so sure," said Joe. "She probably knows him better than anyone. 'Going on crusade' may be his secret code word for 'switching sides'."

Maya thought about this. "It's funny, now you mention it. She looked seriously scared when she heard the news and insisted that he was returned. I thought she was frightened of losing him. But maybe… maybe she was scared he might show up again side by side with Athelbane – her brother's enemy."

The atmosphere in Castle Cranston grew steadily more and more tense over the following days as scouts reported the rapid approach of Athelbane's forces. The castle's knights spent all their days training, and food was stockpiled in readiness for the coming siege. The guards patrolling the walls each night were doubled in number, but even this could not prevent a steady trickle of desertions.

On the positive side, Sir William showed signs of making a full recovery. By the third day, he was able to get up for short periods and even managed to join his father on a visit to the barracks for an inspection of the soldiers. It greatly boosted their morale to see him up and about.

As Joe escorted his master back to his bedchamber, Sir William turned and said: "You know, lad, we're going to need every fit man available in the coming battle. I can see that injury to your leg is looking better now, so that includes you. Can you handle a sword?"

"No…er… my liege," admitted Joe. Then he remembered a skill he'd acquired while camping out in the forest near his home village of Charlton Abbas, and added: "The bow and arrow is my preferred weapon."

"Good," said Sir William. "I've no doubt that will come in handy when the time comes."

* * *

That same morning, Maya was in Lady Hamilton's boudoir, helping her dress. Lady Hamilton was always very formal, ordering Maya to do this and that and never asking her opinion, for example about what to wear.

However, underneath her frosty surface, Maya felt that Lady Hamilton was a kind person. Maya wished they could have a normal conversation, but she wasn't too sure about the rules of a medieval castle. Was a lady-in-waiting basically just a servant – someone who obeyed orders without question? Or could she and her lady be a bit more friendly than that? She so wanted to plead Joanna's case to Lady Hamilton in the hope that she might be persuaded to free the girl – but if Maya went about it the wrong way, she might end up being sent to the dungeon herself.

In the end, she decided her only hope was to give it a try.

She was combing Lady Hamilton's hair when an opportunity arose.

"You have beautiful hair, my lady," she ventured. It was true – Lady Hamilton's hair was long and dark with just a few strands of silvery grey that caught the light.

"Thank you, child. You comb it well. You have a more sensitive touch than the last girl."

"You mean… Joanna?"

"Aye. But you would do well not to speak her name under this roof. The wretched little thief has, by her deeds, brought down a curse that may be the ruin of us all."

Maya took a deep breath. *This was her chance…*

"I don't believe she stole the chalice, my lady."

Did Lady Hamilton stiffen, just a little? Maya continued to comb her hair as if nothing had happened.

"Why do you say that?" asked Lady Hamilton after a moment.

Maya let out a quiet sigh of relief. She didn't sound angry at all – merely curious. Perhaps Lady Hamilton *could* be an ally.

Over the next few minutes, Maya told her everything: about her secret visit to Joanna's cell and Joanna's story about what had really happened, and the girl's suspicion of the chaplain.

As she talked, she began braiding her lady's hair and coiling it around her ears in the way she had been shown.

Maya explained how she'd timed the walk from the kitchen to the chapel and proved that it would have been impossible for Joanna to make that journey and steal the chalice before the chaplain saw her. "Perhaps he saw someone else," she concluded. "Or perhaps he made the whole thing up so that Joanna would be blamed for his crime."

Lady Hamilton did not speak for a while. Finally, without turning around, she said: "Fetch me my linen veil, child."

Maya went to the wardrobe and fetched the veil, decorated with beads, and began fastening it to Lady Hamilton's hair. It bothered her that the lady hadn't responded at all to what she'd just said. The silence made her so nervous, she dropped a whole box of pins on the floor.

As she stooped to tidy them up, Lady Hamilton stood and turned to face her. Her brown eyes looked deeply into Maya's. There was softness there, but also a cool authority. "Dear girl," she said, "what you did that night was both dangerous and ill-advised. I would not have been able to protect you if you had been caught in your… investigations. That girl, your predecessor, is not trustworthy – she is a thief and a liar. She simply told you a story in an attempt to save her own skin."

Maya was saddened to hear these words. "But why would she steal the chalice?" she blurted. "Jo… Sorry, I mean the *girl* doesn't seem the greedy type."

Lady Hamilton pursed her lips. A shadow seemed to pass across her face. "She may have been in league with others," she said pensively. "There are dark forces at work in this castle – powerful, dangerous people who want the chalice for their own purposes. I urge you, for your own safety, to forget all about this business, child. No good will come of it. I have no doubt these people would stop at nothing to prevent the truth from coming out. Pay no more mind to these fancies, and concentrate on your work."

With that, Lady Hamilton swept from the room.

* * *

That night, Joe lay restlessly in his bed, thinking about the coming battle. The distant thunder in the hills sounded like approaching battle drums.

All of a sudden, a much louder sound grabbed his attention: a clatter of horses' hooves in the courtyard. Who could be arriving at such an hour? He got out of bed and ran to the window. Under the pale moonlight, he saw an armoured knight on a black horse trotting across the rainswept courtyard towards the stable block. He carried a blue shield with a gold lion painted in its centre.

Joe had seen that symbol before.

Sir James had returned!

Joe clutched the window ledge as his mind raced. Perhaps Sir James had heard that Sir William was still alive – he might have captured one of Lord Robert's scouts and forced the information out of him. Now he'd returned to kill him.

Joe wanted to warn Sir William. But first he had to make sure that his fears were justified. He crept out of the room into the passage outside. With the wall torches doused, the darkness was total. He waited, back pressed against the cold stone wall, hoping he'd got it all wrong. Perhaps Sir James really had gone on crusade and then got cold feet and decided to come home. If that was the case, then after stabling his horse, Sir James would head straight to his bedchamber on the ground floor. There should be no footsteps in this part of the castle.

These thoughts were interrupted by a sound – a hollow, echoing sound – that made him stiffen with fear. Heavy footsteps… coming up the stairwell.

What should he do? Warn Sir William? But the poor man was still weak with illness. He'd be half asleep and had no armour or sword to defend himself with.

He wouldn't stand a chance.

No, it was up to Joe to protect his master. He swallowed. Somehow he would have to find the courage to do this. But first he needed a weapon. He remembered seeing a suit of armour further down the hall, beyond the stairwell. A sword was clasped in its gauntlets. Joe dashed towards it. Oily torchlight flickered against the wall of the stairwell as he passed it. He found the armour and pulled the sword from its grasp just as Sir James emerged into the passageway and began making his way towards Sir William's room.

Joe was about to approach him when the door beside him suddenly flew open. It led to Lady Hamilton's boudoir, where Maya slept. Joe stared in bewilderment as a panting figure staggered from the room, pushed past him and ran down the corridor.

* * *

A few minutes earlier, Maya had been quietly sleeping in the little bedchamber. In her dream, she was back home at Mycroft Place. It was morning. The sun was shining. Her father was bringing her breakfast in bed. "Good morning, my darling!" he smiled, setting down the tray on her bedside table.

Then the room darkened. Her father's face changed into the face of the steward. He reached down, placed his thin fingers around her neck and started squeezing. Maya began to choke. She grabbed at the hands but couldn't remove them.

Her eyes opened. The crushing tightness around her neck was real! Someone was crouching over her in the darkness, throttling the life out of her. She tried to scream, but couldn't make a sound. She tried to gasp for air, but could feel herself weakening. Her hand fell to the floor. Her fingers touched something hard and sharp there – one of the pins she'd dropped that morning! She grasped it between thumb and forefinger and, with the last of her strength, drove it into the side of her attacker.

There was a yelp of pain, and the tightness around her throat eased.

Maya knew this was her chance. Before the strangler could recover, she punched upwards as hard as she could. She struck a nose or cheek and heard a sharp cry. The figure tried to hit back with a strike at her face, but Maya blocked it and threw another punch towards the stomach area.

Her attacker, who probably hadn't encountered someone with tae kwon do training before, gasped for air and rolled on to the floor. Maya watched the figure rise and dash from the room. She forced herself out of bed, staggering to the door.

She could hear the receding footsteps of her attacker disappearing down the corridor. Through blurred eyes, she saw a boy standing in front of her, sword in hand.

"Joe?" she breathed, feeling her legs give way.

"Maya, what happened?" Joe rushed to support her.

"Quick!" she rasped. "That way! You have to go after him! He tried to strangle me."

Joe stared at her, wide-eyed. "But… Sir William," he began. Turning in the opposite direction, towards his master's bedchamber, he saw Sir James heading inside.

Chapter 9

Besieged!

Joe felt paralysed, unsure what to do.

"Go on!" wheezed Maya, pushing him in the direction of her attacker.

Decision made for him, he set off down the corridor after the strangler. Skidding around a sharp bend in the passage, he almost collided with a figure coming the other way.

"Where do you think you're going in such haste?" came a stern female voice.

Joe saw it was Lady Hamilton, dressed in her nightgown, and she did not look happy.

"I-I'm sorry," he stuttered. "I was…. Did you happen to see someone running along this corridor just a few seconds ago?"

"No, I saw no one," she said. "I've only just now stepped out of my room. I was on my way to see…. Ah, there you are, child."

Maya had come stumbling into view.

"Would you go and fetch me some water. I'm feeling thirsty. Be quick about it."

"She was attacked," said Joe.

"Attacked?" cried Lady Hamilton. "By whom?"

"I don't know," croaked Maya, feeling her throat.

"Foolish child. It was just a nightmare, I expect. Go and get yourself some fresh air, then come and see me in my room. As for you, young man…."

But Joe was already gone.

* * *

Joe burst into Sir William's room, sword raised and ready to strike. To his astonishment, he found Sir James sitting on Sir William's bed. The two of them were talking quite amiably to each other.

When he saw Joe, sword poised above his head, Sir James immediately rose from the bed, hand going to his sword hilt, but Sir William merely smiled. "Rest easy, cousin," he said, "my squire is loyal to the core."

"Are you sure?" said Sir James. "A few nights ago I saw him creeping about suspiciously. Thought he might be a spy for Athelbane. He's lucky I didn't kill him on the spot."

"He got me thinking you might be the same," said Sir William.

"What?" cried Sir James.

"The night I was poisoned, he told me he saw you loitering in the kitchen earlier."

Sir James's face darkened. "I was checking something with cook, that was all."

Sir William nodded. Turning to Joe, he said: "Put down your sword, lad. Sir James is on our side." Joe relaxed and began to breathe freely again. "He's also my spy," continued Sir William. "On my orders, he's been to Athelbane's camp and brought me valuable information about the plans and strategies of our enemy. This was a completely secret operation. No one was told, not even the steward or Lady Hamilton. After all, Athelbane may well have a spy in the castle.... James, do go on. What else did you learn?"

* * *

When Maya emerged on to the roof of the North Tower, the sky was still dark, with just the faintest blush of dawn illuminating the clouds in the east. She took a deep breath of cold air, and her throat immediately felt better. Then she noticed that, to the north, the hills were aglow with a different kind of light: countless torches lined the horizon – a moving forest of flame that turned the sky a smoky red. A faint thud of drums disturbed the air: *tap-tap-tap… tap-tap-tap*. And beneath the torchlight, she glimpsed the silhouettes of armoured men and horses. As she watched, this smouldering sea of black, gleaming metal gradually spilled over the crests of the hills towards the castle like a slow cascade of volcanic lava.

Athelbane's army was coming!

* * *

Lady Hamilton took the news of the army's approach remarkably calmly. Only the tight set of her lips betrayed the tension she had to be feeling. "Dress me, child," she said. "This… this green dress today, I think."

When Maya had finished dressing her, Lady Hamilton asked for her black veil. "You'll find it in that chest over there." Maya rummaged through the piles of clothing. Instead of the veil, her eyes lit on something unexpected. Her heart nearly stopped when she realized what it was.

She quickly stuffed what she had found into the broad sleeve of her tunic. "Yes, my lady," she said, searching for and locating the veil.

Once Maya had pinned the veil in place, Lady Hamilton told her to take down a letter. Trembling with excitement over what she had found, Maya seated herself at the writing desk and pulled a fresh parchment from the drawer. The letter was addressed to someone called John, and it was full of affectionate talk about how much she missed him and how they would soon be together – Maya felt embarrassed just having to write such intimate stuff. She struggled, as always, with the goose-feather quill, and had to keep stopping to dip it in ink or to resharpen the nib with a knife.

As she wrote, another part of Maya's mind was trying to make sense of what she'd just discovered.

When the letter was finished, she handed it to her lady for signing. Unusually, Lady Hamilton added a few words of her own above her signature. She wrote:

Fare thee well gentle sir. I shall not rest easy in body or mind until I know that you are safe.
  Your loving
  Ada

Maya stared at Lady Hamilton's handwriting. There was something oddly familiar about it. The "F" in "Fare" was strangely formed. She was sure she'd seen the same letter written like that somewhere before.

Lady Hamilton rolled up the parchment and dripped wax on the scroll to seal it. "Take this to the marshal in the stable block," she instructed, pressing her ring to the wax to give the letter her personal seal. "Tell him to take it to the tavern in Ochterhallan, where someone will come and collect it."

"I will, my lady," said Maya, hurrying off with the message.

A chill, grey dawn greeted her as she crossed the courtyard on her way to the stables. The dull rhythmic beat of Athelbane's drums had now been joined by a bell urgently clanging from the castle belfry, warning everyone that the enemy was nearly at the gates. Sleepy-eyed servants were scurrying about. Foot soldiers were doing their drills. Archers were assembling on the walls and turrets.

Maya caught sight of Joe on the far side of the courtyard, bow in hand, heading into one of the towers. She ran over to him. "Hey cuz!"

"Maya," he said, stopping. "Looks as if the siege is about to start." He seemed anxious yet grimly determined.

"Can I talk to you a sec?"

Joe glanced towards the turret. "I'm expected up on the walls."

"Please, Joe. This'll be quick."

He placed his bow across his back and followed her into a quiet alley between the turret wall and a blacksmith's workshop.

She took out Lady Hamilton's letter and broke the seal with her thumbnail.

"Hey, won't you get into trouble for that?" he said.

Maya shrugged. "The castle's going to fall today unless we can solve this mystery. I don't think we've got time to worry about a broken seal." She passed it to him. "Does the handwriting at the bottom look familiar to you?"

Joe nodded immediately. "Of course," he said. "Especially that 'F'."

"Where have we seen it before?"

"Quickly, come with me and I'll show you!" exclaimed Joe.

* * *

The chapel was empty when they got there. Joe ran to the altar and opened the small, jewelled box where the chaplain kept the black parchment containing the curse. He carefully unfurled it. They both scanned the gold-inked words. The first word of the second line contained that curiously formed "F"…

From within these walls

"Maybe that's just the way everyone writes in this era," said Joe.

Maya shook her head. "No, I've seen letters from people she writes to, and I've seen notes to her from the steward and Sir James and the chaplain. None of them write their *F*s like that."

"Assuming you're right, why would Lady Hamilton have written the curse?" Joe wondered.

"Because she wants to destroy her brother and his son, so that her own son Sir James can be the new Earl of Cranston."

"Wait a minute," said Joe. "You're going way too fast for me. Are you saying she was behind *everything*? The curse? The theft of the chalice? The poisoning of Sir William? The murder attempts on you and me?"

Maya nodded. "Everything."

"And you're basing all this on what evidence? A dodgy 'F'?"

"And this," said Maya, tugging a wig from out of her sleeve with a flourish.

"A wig?"

"I found an auburn wig in her chest earlier. Remember that the chaplain said he saw a red-haired woman leaving the chapel on the day the chalice was stolen? I think Lady Hamilton disguised herself as Joanna when she stole the chalice."

"Okay," said Joe. "That's not bad. Anything else?"

"The footprint in the library. It was small, remember?"

Joe shuddered at the memory. "You think it was Lady Hamilton up there, pushing that statue on top of me?"

"Yes, I do."

"What are you doing here, child?"

Lady Hamilton's voice rang out across the chapel, sending a cold finger of fear down Maya's spine. She whirled around, quickly hiding the wig once more and passing the letter to Joe behind her back.

"N-Nothing, my lady," she stammered.

"Have you delivered my letter to the marshal?"

"Er, yes, my lady."

Lady Hamilton came further into the room, suspicion creasing her marble-smooth forehead. "What are you doing by the altar? Only the chaplain is allowed there. And why is that box open? Isn't that where the curse is kept?"

"S-Sir William asked me to fetch it for him!" stammered Joe, holding up the black parchment. Sheer desperation was forcing his brain to invent a story. "He's… he's on the battlements now, and this curse has got the men into such a state, he says he wants to burn it in front of them. It's the only way he can get them to fight."

Joe let out a breath. His cock-and-bull story had actually made a kind of sense! He glanced at Maya, who was gazing at him in open admiration.

Lady Hamilton glared at him for a moment longer, then seemed to relent. "Well, don't let me keep you," she said. "Go up there, now." Joe nodded and left. Lady Hamilton turned to Maya. "We've been ordered to remain in our rooms in the keep for the duration of the siege. It will be safer for us there."

"Yes, my lady," curtsied Maya.

With that, Lady Hamilton turned and swept out of the chapel. Maya was following her when Joe, who'd been lurking in the shadows just outside, grabbed her arm. "That green dress she was wearing. It's got gold in the sleeves" he whispered.

"What about it?"

From his pocket, Joe drew out a twist of green and gold thread.

"Where did you find that?" asked Maya.

"Hanging from the candle holder at the altar, the day we got here – the day the chalice was stolen. She must have snagged it on there while she was... stealing the chalice." He stared at her. "I think you may be on to something here, Maya. We'll go and see the constable. Now."

Chapter 10

The Thief Uncovered

They found him on the roof of the barbican. Archers were kneeling at the battlements, arrows at the ready. As Joe took in the view to the north, his mouth suddenly went very dry. It was his first sighting of the enemy. Athelbane's forces stood before Castle Cranston in massed ranks, covering the valley like a dark carpet. There were thousands of them, arrayed in perfect formation, their iron armour glinting in the early morning sun. Colourful banners carried by mounted troops rippled in the stiff breeze, which suddenly felt very cold on Joe's skin.

"Are ye goin' to stand their gawpin' laddie, or will ye get to your station?" the constable yelled at Joe. Then his eye fell on Maya. "What's a servin' lass doin' up here? Get back tae the keep wi' yer."

"Sir, we need to speak to you about an urgent matter," said Joe.

The constable looked as if he might just explode. "I'd love tae know what could be more urgent than *that*!" he bellowed, gesturing at Athelbane's army.

"We know who stole the chalice," said Maya.

"Aye," he said. "So do I. Ah'm just waitin' for her confession."

"It wasn't Joanna, sir," said Maya. "It was…." She glanced around. "Can we talk somewhere else?"

"This had better be worth it!" sighed the constable, ushering them down some steps to a room full of winches and chains – the controls for the portcullis.

Joe and Maya quickly detailed the evidence they had assembled against Lady Hamilton.

The constable pretended to give it some thought. "So, let me see," he said, stroking his beard. "Ye have a footprint, a wig, a piece o' thread and an oddly shaped 'F'. And on that basis you expect me tae walk up to Lady Ada Hamilton, sister of the Earl who I've served loyally these past twenty years, and accuse her of theft and attempted murder? Have ye ta'en leave of yer senses? D'ye want tae see me hung, drawn and quartered?"

"No," said Joe quickly. "We've got a much better plan than that…."

* * *

Half an hour later, Maya returned to Lady Hamilton's rooms. She found her in her bedchamber, gazing through the window at the men assembled on the walls. She turned as Maya came in. "We'd better close up these shutters, child. The battle will soon begin."

"Of course, my lady," said Maya. "Just one thing, though, before I do that...." She pulled out the auburn wig. "Could you explain *this*, my lady. Did you use it, by any chance, to disguise yourself as Joanna while you stole the chalice?"

Lady Hamilton's lips fell open in surprise. Apart from that, she didn't move a muscle.

Maya held up the green-and-gold thread. "And could you also explain how this, which matches the dress you're now wearing, could have got snagged on the candle holder at the chapel altar on the day of the theft? You told us yourself that only the chaplain is allowed by the altar." Maya smiled as she watched the anger building in Lady Hamilton's eyes. "And may I also ask why you're standing in that crooked way, with your hand above your hip? Could it be because of a wound from a hairpin by any chance?"

Hearing this, Lady Hamilton's calm expression suddenly warped into a scowl of pure hatred. "You vile, treacherous creature!" she hissed. "You may have worked all this out, but you won't live to repeat it to a single soul!" As she said this, she pulled a knife from beneath her pillow and ran at Maya, eyes red with murderous fury.

Suddenly, the curtain to the adjoining boudoir was quickly swept aside and out stepped the constable. He grabbed Lady

Hamilton's wrist as the knife was descending towards Maya. White with shock, the lady let the knife clatter to the floor.

"Why, constable!" she said, attempting an innocent smile. "Please, allow me to explain…."

"You've explained yerself well enough, your ladyship," said the constable. "Now hand over the chalice!"

* * *

Athelbane's archers stood in their lines, facing the castle, bows at the ready. A figure passed along the line with a torch, igniting each arrow in turn. When all the arrows were lit, the archers raised their bows to the sky and pulled the strings taut. "Fire!" someone bellowed, and a hundred flaming bolts soared upwards, arcing through the air towards the walls and turrets of the castle.

Joe, kneeling at the battlements, tried not to think about anything except firing his own next arrow. As the first bolts landed, he heard men nearby crying out, and saw fires break out along the castle walkways. The air stank of burning pitch and shimmered with heat.

Joe quickly fell into a rhythm: *Notch… Draw… Aim… Fire… Notch… Draw… Aim… Fire*. With each firing, he and his fellow defenders created a hailstorm of arrows. Many found their mark, piercing armour and chain mail and felling scores of enemy foot soldiers.

Yet Athelbane's army was enormous, and it kept on coming like an unstoppable tide. Another volley of blazing arrows erupted into the sky, igniting fresh fires on the battlements and in the stables and exercise yard. Meanwhile, attacking soldiers pushed wooden towers against the castle walls. Inside these towers were ladders to scale the defences.

Gloom pervaded the hearts of the defenders when they saw this. "It's the curse," they whispered to each other. "We lost the chalice, and now we're sure to lose our lives."

But then, in the midst of this desperate scene, Sir William arrived on the barbican. He was pale and thin, still weak from the poisoning, yet a new energy and confidence seemed to be driving him. Something golden glittered in his hand. He held it up so that a ray of sun, lancing through the battle-smoke, shone off its surface.

"Behold, the Holy Chalice of St Ninian!" he cried, his voice cracking. "It has returned! The curse is lifted! We shall win this fight! Castle Cranston shall not fall!"

The men clamoured to observe the beautiful, sacred object for themselves. When they saw it, they gave an almighty cheer. Word quickly spread around the walls and turrets, prompting more loud hurrahs.

Joe took heart along with everyone else. It hadn't taken the constable long to persuade Lady Hamilton to hand over the stolen relic. He hoped its recovery would be enough to turn the battle around. The situation was not looking hopeful: he could already see hordes of enemy soldiers clambering up the ladders inside the siege towers towards the battlements.

Defenders frantically poured boiling water, heavy stones and hot sand through the "murder holes" in the floor of the barbican roof. This knocked some attackers from the ladders, but more kept arriving from below.

Joe could only watch in anguish as the first attackers surged over the walls, rushing at the defenders with their swords. They even made it on to the barbican, the most heavily defended tower, and the air shook with cries and groans and the clink of clashing swords.

The next hour passed in a blur for Joe as the battle ebbed and flowed around him. Sometimes it seemed as if Athelbane's men were about to take the castle, but then at the last moment they would be pushed back again. At one point, Joe was amazed to see Maya standing on the battlements. She had hitched up her skirts and was performing tae kwondo kicks on the attackers as they leapt on to the wall, sending them tumbling back down again.

She seemed more than a match for any of them until, through the smoke, emerged a giant of a man. He had a straggly beard, wild eyes and a flashing sword blade, and he pushed Maya aside as if she were a rag doll. As the huge warrior leapt on to the barbican roof, he immediately cut down a soldier who dared confront him. Then Sir William stepped forward.

"Withdraw if you value your life, Athelbane!" he growled at the giant. "You're not taking this castle."

"That I am!" roared Athelbane. "And neither you nor your father can stop me!" With that, he threw himself at Sir William, sword cutting and slicing the air as he came.

Despite his illness, Sir William was a formidable swordsman, and he managed to dodge his adversary's assault and then counter-attack with some quick and dangerous moves of his own. Their swords became a blur as they went at each other, swinging, lunging and stabbing. Athelbane sliced at Sir William's neck, and Sir William twisted away and thrust his weapon towards the bigger man's chest.

Soon the fight had captured the attention of everyone on the barbican, including Joe and Maya. No one saw Lady Hamilton, a hood now covering her face, creep silently on to the roof. She stole ever closer to Sir William, her knife concealed beneath her cloak. As he retreated in the face of one of Athelbane's assaults, he came within her range. Lady Hamilton raised her knife.

Joe, suddenly noticing her, took aim with his bow and fired. The arrow pierced her leg. She screamed and fell to the ground, clutching the wound. When he saw this, Athelbane went pale with shock. "Ada!" he cried.

"John, watch out!" screamed Lady Hamilton.

But she was too late. While Athelbane was distracted, Sir William struck. The giant keeled over with a resounding crash.

When news spread of their slain leader, all the spirit went out of the attacking army, and they quickly withdrew from the castle and surrendered.

The constable arrived on the barbican roof a short while later. "Where is she?" he roared. "Where's mah prisoner?"

"Over there," said Sir William, pointing with his sword towards the groaning heap that was his aunt. "Take her to the castle hospital to have that wound dressed," he said. "But let her wait her turn behind every soldier who suffered an injury defending this castle today."

Before she could be taken away, Sir James arrived on the barbican, nursing a shoulder wound. He fought his way through the crowd of soldiers to kneel by his wounded mother. "Why?" he cried. "What were you thinking?"

"I did all this for you," she croaked. "I wanted you to be Earl of Cranston. I was going to marry Athelbane. Join his lands to ours."

Sir James shook his head in disbelief. "But you should have known, I would never betray my uncle and cousin."

"You were always too soft, my son," she muttered as the stretcher bearers carried her off.

When the constable learned how close she'd come to killing Sir William, he was overcome with shame. "I was distracted by the battle, sire," he sobbed. "But I shouldna let the prisoner out o' mah sight!"

"Fear not," said Sir William. "My squire was equal to the occasion. He shot her before she could do any damage…. Speaking of which, where is the boy, and that girl he's always with?"

The steward emerged on to the barbican roof, wiping ash and soot from his otherwise spotless tunic. "That pair of wretches are always running off and evading their duties, sire," he said. "But I shall find them for you."

"I wouldn't bother, steward," said Sir William with a wistful smile. "Something tells me, we won't be seeing them again."

* * *

When Joe and Maya arrived back in the present day, they found themselves on the battlements of Castle Cranston. Not only was the castle still standing, it was now a beautifully preserved tourist attraction. Making their way down the steps to the great hall, they found a huge tapestry on the wall depicting the famous siege of 1270. Just visible on the battlements were two children, a boy firing a bow and a girl kicking enemy soldiers this way and that.

"I've often wondered who they might be," said a voice nearby. They turned to see a young man standing next to them, peering at the tapestry. He had a slim face and stubble on his cheeks. His startlingly pale blue eyes looked from them to the tapestry and back again, a quizzical look on his face.

Joe suddenly remembered where he'd seen him before. "Hey, aren't you that tramp we met here when this place was just a...." He trailed off, realizing how ridiculous he must sound.

The man gave him a puzzled smile. "Tramp?" he said. "Do I look like a tramp then?" Actually, he was smartly dressed in a black jacket, kilt and bow tie.

"I'm sorry," said Joe. "I must have made a mistake."

"You made a mistake coming to this part of the castle, too, laddie. This is my private quarters. Perhaps I ought to introduce myself. My name is Lord Robert Mackenzie, twenty-ninth Earl of Cranston – and I *own* this castle."

THE END

FICTI●N EXPRESS

THE READERS TAKE CONTROL!

Have you ever wanted to change the course of a plot, change a character's destiny, tell an author what to write next?

Well, now you can!

'The Curse of Castle Cranston' was originally written for the award-winning interactive e-book website Fiction Express.

Fiction Express e-books are published in gripping weekly episodes. At the end of each episode, readers are given voting options to decide where the plot goes next. They vote online and the winning vote is then conveyed to the author who writes the next episode, in real time, according to the readers' most popular choice.

www.fictionexpress.co.uk

WINNER
Education Resources
Award for Innovation

133

FICTION EXPRESS

TALK TO THE AUTHORS

The Fiction Express website features a blog where readers can interact with the authors while they are writing. An exciting and unique opportunity!

FANTASTIC TEACHER RESOURCES

Each weekly Fiction Express episode comes with a PDF of teacher resources packed with ideas to extend the text.

"The teaching resources are fab and easily fill a whole week of literacy lessons!"
Rachel Humphries, teacher at Westacre Middle School

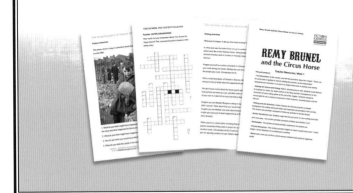

FICTI●N EXPRESS

The Time Detectives:
The Mystery of Maddie Musgrove
by Alex Woolf

When Joe Smallwood goes to stay with his Uncle Theo and cousin Maya life seems dull, until he finds a strange smartphone nestling beside a gravestone. The phone enables Joe and Maya to become time-travelling detectives and takes them on an exciting adventure back to Victorian times. Can they prove maidservant Maddie Musgrove's innocence? Can they save her from the gallows?

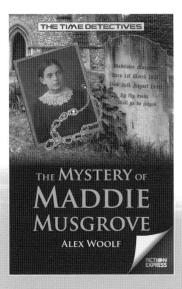

ISBN 978-1-78322-459-3

FICTI●N EXPRESS

The Time Detectives:
The Disappearance of Danny Doyle
by Alex Woolf

When the Time Detectives, Joe and Maya, stumble upon an old house in the middle of a wood, its occupant has a sad tale to tell. Michael was evacuated to Dorset during World War II with his twin brother, Danny. While there, Danny mysteriously disappeared and was never heard from again. Can Joe and Maya succeed where the police failed, journey back to 1941 and trace Michael's missing brother?

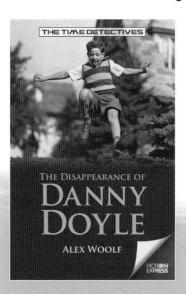

ISBN 978-1-78322-458-6

FICTI🗨N EXPRESS

My Cousin Faustina
by Bea Davenport

Jez is horrified to find a strange girl sitting in his kitchen when he gets home from school. His parents claim she is a distant cousin, but Jez senses something odd about her. Just what dark secret is Faustina hiding?

In his quest to find out, Jez learns the true value of family and friendship.

ISBN 978-1-78322-539-2